For information address Disney Press, 114 Fifth Avenue, New York, New York 10011-5690. Volume three of Disney Classics Classic Library.

Printed in China

First Edition
1 3 5 7 9 10 8 6 4 2

T425-2382-5-12278
ISBN 978-1-4231-7939-9

For more Disney Press fun, visit www.disneybooks.com

This book was printed on paper created from a sustainable source.

Disney PRESS
New York

ONE CHRISTMAS MORNING, Jim Dear gave his wife, Darling, a very special present. It was wrapped in a box and tied with a pink ribbon.

When Darling opened it, a tiny cocker spaniel puppy peeped out at her.

"How sweet!" cried Darling, "what a perfectly beautiful little lady."

And that was how Lady got her name.

When Lady was six months old, she was given a beautiful blue collar. She was so proud, she rushed out to show it to her friends Jock and Trusty. Jock was a small black Scottish terrier. Trusty was a big brown bloodhound. He had once been a famous police dog, but now he was old and he'd lost most of his sense of smell.

"My, you're a full-grown lady now!" said Jock.

Lady felt that she was the luckiest, happiest dog in the whole world.

A few weeks later, Jock and Trusty found Lady lying by her water bowl. She looked very sad.

"What's wrong, lassie?" asked Jock.

Lady explained that Jim Dear and Darling seemed upset with her—but she didn't know why.

"I wouldn't worry," Jock said. "Darling is expecting a wee bairn."

Lady looked confused.

"He means a baby," Trusty explained.

"Oh!" said Lady, still confused. "What's a baby?"

"A baby," Jock began, "is a cute little bundle of—"

But before he could finish, a voice behind him said, ". . . trouble."

Lady turned around to see who had spoken. Walking toward her was a scruffy but handsome dog called Tramp. "Remember, when a baby moves in, the dog moves out!" he warned.

At last the baby came. The whole family gathered around the cradle, including Lady, who thought the baby was wonderful.

"We're going to be all right," she said to herself. "Tramp was wrong. Nothing has really changed."

A few months later, Jim and Darling went away to visit friends. Aunt Sarah came to look after the baby, and she brought her two Siamese cats with her.

The cats were sly and mischievous. They raced through the house frightening the canary, ripping the curtains, and tipping over the goldfish bowl!

"What's all this?" cried Aunt Sarah when she saw the mess. "It must have been that dog!"

The cats rolled on the floor, pretending Lady had attacked them.

"Bad dog!" Aunt Sarah said to Lady. "Just you wait!"

Aunt Sarah took Lady straight to the pet shop to have a muzzle put on.

Lady struggled as the shopkeeper fastened it over her face. Panicking, she tore out of the shop and raced down the street. She had to get away from Aunt Sarah!

As Lady dashed across the road, she was nearly knocked down by a car. Terrified, she ran into a side street. Suddenly, a pack of stray dogs jumped out and began chasing her.

Lady fled down an alley to escape, but a huge fence blocked her way. She was trapped!

Just as the dogs were about to attack her, Tramp jumped over the fence. He was a fierce fighter and quickly scared off the other dogs.

Tramp walked back to Lady, who was shaking with fear.

"Oh! You poor kid," he said, looking at her muzzle. "Come on. We've got to get that thing off."

Tramp led Lady to a nearby zoo, where they soon spotted a beaver who happily bit through Lady's muzzle. In a second it dropped off and Lady was free again!

As the stars began to twinkle in the sky, Tramp said, "Come on, it's supper time."

He led Lady to the back door of Tony's Italian restaurant. Tony's chef, Joe, was a friend of Tramp's, and brought the couple a plate of spaghetti.

While Tony and Joe played soft romantic music, Lady and Tramp shared a delicious meal.

What a wonderful night, Lady thought. Suddenly, her lips met Tramp's. They were both eating the same strand of spaghetti! Lady blushed and the two dogs gazed dreamily at each other. They were falling in love.

After supper, Tramp took Lady for a stroll in the park. Soon, the two dogs fell asleep together under the stars.

The next morning, Lady woke with a start. She had forgotten about the baby. She needed to go home to care for him!

As they approached Lady's home, Tramp spotted a henhouse. "Follow me," he shouted.

Tramp began chasing the chickens around the farmyard. Feathers flew everywhere! Suddenly, there was a loud bang.

"Come on!" shouted Tramp as he squeezed under a fence. "That's the signal to get going!"

Tramp and Lady dashed around the corner. They splashed through a stream and jumped over ditches. Tramp raced ahead. When he turned around, Lady was nowhere to be seen. She had been caught by a dogcatcher!

Poor Lady was taken to the dog pound. Lady's eyes filled with tears as the door of her cell clanged shut behind her.

Before long, Aunt Sarah picked Lady up from the dog pound. She was very upset with Lady for running away. When they got home, she chained Lady to a doghouse in the backyard and yelled, "Stay there! Don't you make any noise, or I'll send you back to that pound!"

Lady was too miserable to do anything but lie there. Even her good friends, Trusty and Jock, couldn't make her feel better.

Soon Tramp came trotting into the garden with a big, juicy bone for Lady. But Lady was angry with him.

"It was all your fault," she cried.

Tramp didn't understand. "What do you mean?" he asked.

But Lady was too hurt to answer him. She just turned away and put her nose in the air.

"It wasn't really my fault," Tramp said miserably. "I thought you were following me."

When Lady refused to answer, Tramp set down her bone and left.

Lady felt so unhappy that she lay down in the kennel and cried. Suddenly, she noticed two eyes glinting in the shadows. A huge rat was scurrying toward the house! Lady barked and tried to chase it away, but her chain held her back.

Luckily, Tramp heard Lady barking. He ran back to see what was wrong.

"It's a rat!" cried Lady. "It ran up the side of the house and into the baby's room."

In a flash, Tramp was inside the house, up the stairs, and through the nursery door. The rat was about to jump into the baby's crib when Tramp leaped at it. There was a terrible fight. Finally, Tramp trapped the rat and killed it. Outside, Lady managed to pull free from her chain. She raced inside the house and upstairs to the nursery.

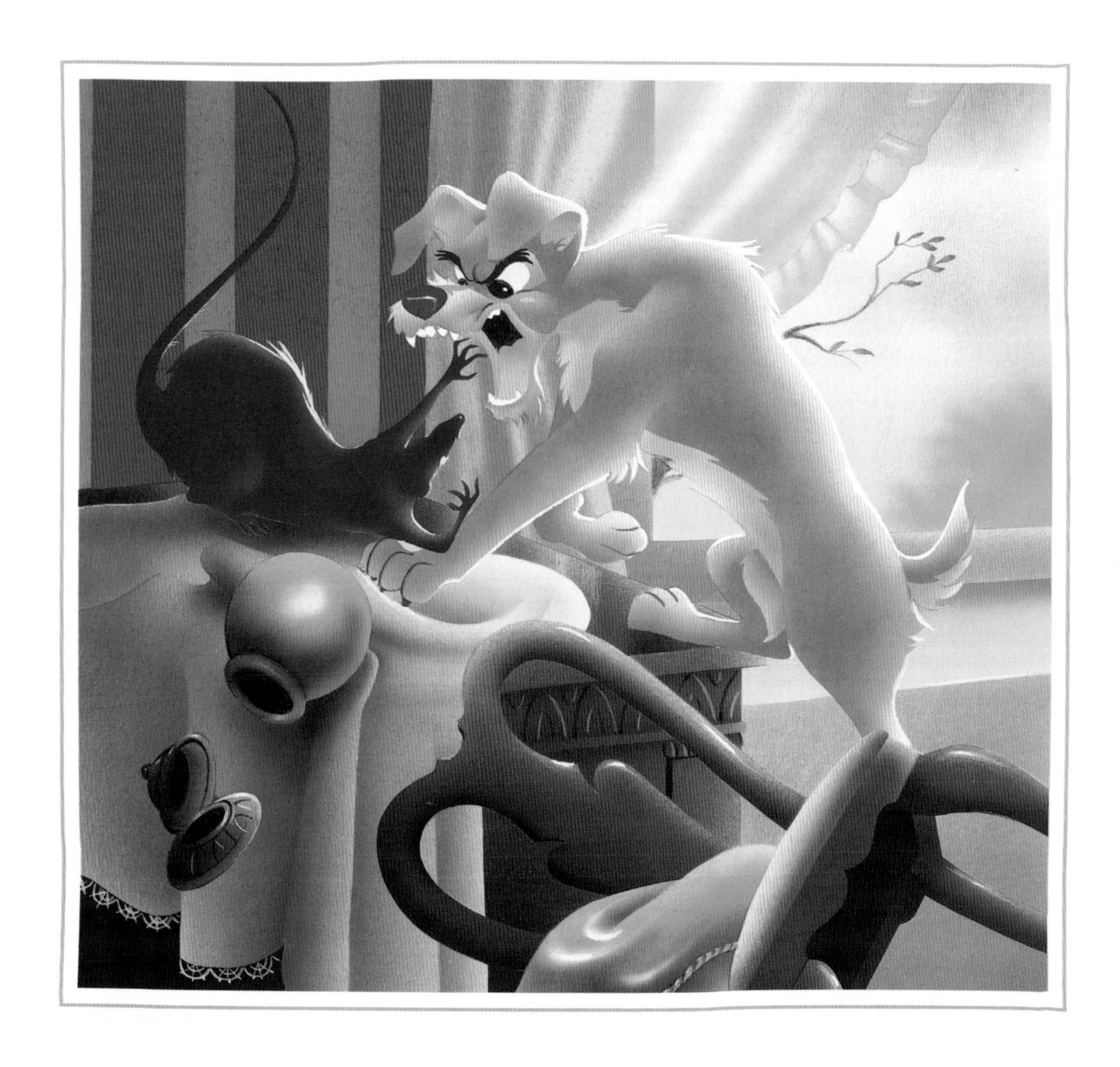

Aunt Sarah heard the commotion and came rushing into the nursery. She was sure that Lady and Tramp were responsible for the mess.

"You vicious brutes!" she shouted, pushing Tramp into a cupboard with her broom. Then she dragged Lady downstairs and locked her in a dark, damp cellar.

Aunt Sarah telephoned the dog pound and ordered them to come take Tramp away.

The dogcatcher arrived quickly. Jock and Trusty watched as Tramp was locked in the van.

"I was certain he was no good the moment I saw him," Jock said.

But Trusty wasn't so sure Tramp was to blame.

Inside, a voice called, "Lady! Lady!" Jim and Darling had come home!

Aunt Sarah started to tell them what naughty dogs Tramp and Lady had been, but Jim didn't believe her. Lady was barking and he knew there was something wrong.

"Look! She wants us to follow her upstairs," he said.

They all rushed up to the baby's room, and found Lady barking at the curtain.

"What's the matter, Lady?" they asked.

Jim looked behind the chair and saw the dead rat.

Jock and Trusty heard everything Jim said. They realized that Tramp had saved the baby. The two began following the scent of the dogcatcher's wagon. They were determined to free Tramp.

When they finally caught up with the wagon, Trusty barked at the horses.

"Look out, Trusty!" called Jock. But it was too late. The horses reared in fright, and the wagon crashed onto its side. Trusty was stuck underneath.

Suddenly a taxi drove up with Lady and Jim Dear in it. Lady jumped out and raced over to the wagon.

"Tramp, are you all right?" she called through the netting.

Tramp was safe, but Trusty had been crushed by the wheel.

"He needs a doctor," said Jock. And they took Trusty to the hospital.

A few months later, Jock and Trusty came to visit Lady and Tramp. Jim Dear knew that Tramp had saved the baby and had taken him in. Now Lady and Tramp were the proud parents of four little puppies.

"They've got their mother's eyes," said Trusty. He looked fondly at three of the tiny puppies.

"Aye, but there's a bit of their father in them, too," said Jock, trying to stop the fourth puppy from chewing his coat!

Lady and Tramp smiled. They were very proud of their new family.

Tramp looked down and thought of how his life had changed in a year. He couldn't be happier. And he knew they would all live happily ever after.